Charlie's

written by Pam Holden
illustrated by Richard Hoit

Our cousin Charlie came to visit us.
He lives in a country far, far away.
We went to the airport to meet him.

Charlie had never been to our country.
We wanted to show him all the
fun things to do where we live.

On the first day, we went to the beach.
Charlie liked swimming in the sea and
jumping through the big waves.
He helped us make a sand castle.

"I would like to learn to ride on a
surfboard," he said.

On the second day, we went to the
park to watch a game of soccer.
We cheered when the players got a goal.
Charlie had never had hot dogs before.

"I would like to play for that team,"
he told us.

On the third day, we took Charlie
high up in the mountains.
He had never played in snow before.
He helped us make a snowman, and
we had a snowball fight.

"I would like to learn how to ski," said Charlie.

On the fourth day, we took Charlie
to the lake to catch some fish.
Then he helped us sail our model boat.
We watched a big sailboat going by.

"I'd like to learn how to sail like that,"
Charlie told us.

The next day, we went to visit a farm.
Charlie had never seen sheep before.
We helped the farmer feed his pigs
and cows and goats.

"I would like to learn to ride a horse,"
said Charlie.

On the last day, we had a barbecue.
Charlie watched Dad cook the food.
"Yum! I'd like to learn how to cook
hamburgers," he said.

We were sad that Charlie was going home to his own country.
"We would like you to stay here longer," we told him.

"I will come back soon," said Charlie.
"I liked my visit to your country.
There are so many fun things to do."